The
Tooth Fairy

The Five Mile Press

Tom had a loose tooth. It fell out while he and his sister Holly were playing in the garden.

"Don't lose it," said Holly. "We'll put it in a glass of water. Then tonight we'll wait for the Tooth Fairy to come and collect it."

So Tom put the tooth in his pocket. But when he looked for it at tea-time it had vanished.

After tea, Tom and Holly took a torch and went into the garden to search for the lost tooth, but it was nowhere to be found. Tired and disappointed, they went to bed.

"Now we'll *never* see the Tooth Fairy," sighed Holly. "Last time, when I lost a tooth, I tried so hard to stay awake, but I couldn't. The Tooth Fairy took my tooth, left some money behind, and was gone. I didn't see a thing!"

That night, the children slept soundly. Just as the sun was rising, Tom was woken by a tinkling in the kitchen. He tip-toed in and saw the Tooth Fairy sitting on the window sill.

"Tom," she said softly, "You must search for your missing tooth — it's very important indeed. If you and Holly can find it, I promise to show you my home in the clouds and tell you why I need your tooth."

So Tom woke up Holly, and together they ran out into the garden. Frantically, they searched for the missing tooth.

At last, they found it, shining white amongst the daisies.

"Hooray!" laughed the Tooth Fairy. "Now I'll take you to Cloudland, just as I promised."

She waved her magic wand, and suddenly Holly and Tom were as small as the Tooth Fairy.

But before they had time to be surprised, she waved her wand again and white doves began to swoop down from the trees. They had golden bridles and red velvet saddles.

"Jump on, Holly!" cried Tom. "We're going for a ride — up into the sky!"

The white doves flew high into the pink dawn sky where amongst the clouds lay a magical land with hills as soft as cotton wool.

They landed beside a beautiful palace surrounded by gardens full of the strangest plants the children had ever seen.

There were silver stars growing like flowers, and tended by pixie gardeners, and moored by a cloud was a boat with rainbow sails.

"Now, Holly and Tom," said the Tooth Fairy, "the stars in the sky eventually grow old and fall down, and the fairies must replace them.

"New stars grow from special star seeds, which are children's baby teeth. That is why when a child's tooth drops out I come down and collect it!"

"But why is my tooth so important?" asked Tom.

"Well," said the Tooth Fairy, "most stars in the sky are silver, but here and there you can see gold ones.

"Now, *your* teeth are very special, Tom, because they will grow into golden stars. And we know an old golden star will fall very soon, and will need to be replaced."

"Look!" cried Holly. "A golden star is falling now!"

"Come, children!" said the Tooth Fairy, taking their hands. "It's time to replace the old golden star. We must hurry and plant Tom's tooth in the sky!"

A silver boat was moored not far from the house. The Tooth Fairy and the children climbed aboard and together they set sail into the sky until they reached the place where the golden star had been.

"Please may I plant my own tooth?" asked Tom.

"Of course," said the Tooth Fairy, and she showed Tom what to do.

The silver boat sailed back to Cloudland, and the Tooth Fairy and the children jumped out onto the clouds.

"Soon you must go home," said the Tooth Fairy, "but first come into my house and have some breakfast."

A bell tinkled and all the pixie gardeners came scampering inside to join them. They all had breakfast together. Then the Tooth Fairy waved her magic wand and…

Tom found he was back in his own bed!

Holly came running into his room.

"Tom!" she said excitedly. "Did we really see the Tooth Fairy last night? Or was it a dream?"

"It's true!" laughed Tom. "The Tooth Fairy took us with her to Cloudland!"

That night Tom and Holly searched the sky for a glittering new golden star.

"Look!" cried Tom, at last. "There it is! That's the one I planted! My very own golden star!"